SPY TOYS
OUT OF CONTROL!

MARK POWERS

ILLUSTRATED BY
TIM WESSON

BLOOMSBURY
LONDON OXFORD NEW YORK NEW DELHI SYDNEY

Bloomsbury Publishing, London, Oxford, New York, New Delhi and Sydney

First published in Great Britain in August 2017 by Bloomsbury Publishing Plc
50 Bedford Square, London WC1B 3DP

www.bloomsbury.com

BLOOMSBURY is a registered trademark of Bloomsbury Publishing Plc

A CIP catalogue record for this book is available from the British Library

ISBN 978 1 4088 7088 4

Printed and bound in Great Britain by CPI Group (UK) Ltd, Croydon CR0 4YY

1 3 5 7 9 10 8 6 4 2

For Sarah Fairchild and Lindsay Spear

With thanks to Jo, Kate, Zöe, Hannah,
Tim, Ian and all at Bloomsbury

CHAPTER ONE

HOG WILD

The enormous hedgehog waddled along the rim of the volcano, chuckling smugly.

This was not your average hedgehog. As a baby, it had fallen into a vat of chemical plant food called Watson's Wicked Wonder-Grow, which had made the creature bigger, stronger and cleverer than any hedgehog that had ever lived. It was also much, much, *much* keener to take over the world.

The hedgehog rubbed its front paws together and cackled as it watched a crane swing into position over the volcano's fiery, bubbling crater. Suspended from the crane was a net containing Mr Alan Sponge (a traffic warden who collected pottery penguins in his spare time), his wife Victoria (a school head teacher and keen amateur cheese-maker), their twin sons, Robin and Kyle (both valuable members of their school's cricket team) and their cat Hobnob (brown with white patches).

The tremendous heat radiating from the crater had already begun to lightly toast the soles of the Sponges' feet, and the acrid stench of sulphur from the volcano's fumes stung their nostrils.

'Please, Professor Doomprickle!' begged Alan Sponge. 'You don't have to kill us! Surely humankind and hedgehogs can learn to live together in peace?' He looked at the

hedgehog with wide, imploring eyes.

'It's too late for that,' snapped Professor Doomprickle. 'You idiots have been feeding the hedgehogs in your garden saucers of bread and milk! That gives us upset tummies! Dog food is far better! Your ill-informed actions have made dozens of hedgehogs sick over the years!'

'I'm sorry!' cried Alan Sponge. 'I never knew! I thought you'd like a nice saucer of –'

'Silence!' boomed Professor Doomprickle, his long spines bristling with anger. 'Well, now it's payback time! First, I shall barbecue you and your family like pork chops! Then people will see Professor Doomprickle means business! Next, I shall create an army of super-hedgehogs like myself and take over the world! And we'll make sure that all the human race has to eat from now on are saucers of yucky old bread and milk! See how you like it!'

He reached for a lever on a large upright control panel nearby and yanked it. There was a clank and a whir, and the net containing the Sponge family began to lower itself slowly towards the fiery pit.

'HELP' 'HELP!'

Professor Doomprickle guffawed loudly and began to film the lowering net on his smartphone.

'You know,' said a squeaky voice, 'if you're filming, you should really hold the phone sideways. You get a much better result in landscape mode.'

'Huh?' Professor Doomprickle turned to find a small, fluffy rabbit standing beside him. It was wearing a neat collared shirt and tie, and had a backpack slung over one shoulder. Standing next to the rabbit were a rag doll and a teddy bear. 'Who the flipping flip are you three?' he exclaimed.

The teddy bear stepped forward. 'We're the people who have come to stop you,' he said in a friendly voice.

The enormous hedgehog threw back his head and laughed at the sky. 'You three pathetic playthings? Stop me? Unlikely, I think!'

The rag doll rolled her eyes. 'Villains – they never listen, do they?'

The teddy bear shrugged. 'We're giving you the option of surrendering peacefully, Professor. Just remember that when you're at the animal hospital. Recovering.'

'Pah!' spat Professor Doomprickle. 'You'll have to catch me first! And even then you'll never stop the Sponges from getting baked!

'STOAT GUARDS, ATTACK!'

6

And with that Professor Doomprickle leaped on to a small motor scooter he'd kept hidden behind the control panel, and roared off down the side of the volcano, chuckling loudly.

A little way off sat five large stoats, who had been playing Top Trumps and not taking much notice of what was going on. But now they leaped into action and advanced on the three newcomers with gruesome snarls and raised claws.

Meanwhile, above the hissing, churning furnace of the volcano, the net containing the Sponge family continued its relentless descent ...

The teddy bear – whose name was Dan – assessed the situation swiftly. 'Arabella,' he barked to the rag doll, 'you deal with the stoats.' Next, he pointed at the rabbit. 'Flax – you stop that walking pine cone Doomprickle. Leave the Sponges to me.'

Arabella punched the palm of her hand with a loud smacking noise. 'My pleasure, furball.' She laughed and ran towards the stoats, yelling battle cries.

Flax opened his backpack and produced a small electronic device with an aerial. He began to push buttons rapidly.

Dan hurried to the control panel. But the hedgehog had locked its levers and it wouldn't let him move the crane. He stared in horror as the Sponge family plunged steadily towards the volcano's blazing mouth. 'Fine,' he muttered. 'We'll do it the *other* way.'

The little teddy bear sprinted towards the base of the towering crane. Using only his paws, he took hold of the crane and bent the vast metal structure as easily as if it were a drinking straw, swinging the Sponge family away from the fearsome pit of the volcano and lowering them gently on to the safety of its slopes. The Sponge family quickly set about freeing themselves from the net's tangles.

'Thank you, little bear!' called Alan Sponge. 'That was astounding!'

The bear waved a modest paw. 'No worries, pal.'

What Alan Sponge didn't know was that Dan was one of a vast range of walking, talking, thinking toys made by a company called Snaztacular Ultrafun. A fault during Dan's manufacture had left him with a thousand times the strength of a normal teddy bear. While this incredible muscle power made him somewhat overqualified to be a child's toy, it did make him terribly good at saving people from peril and catching bad guys.

Meanwhile, Arabella was using her own very special set of skills to tackle the stoat guards. The Sponges watched as she sailed through the air in a great two-footed karate jump. Her right foot connected squarely with the jaw of one stoat, while each of her fists smashed into the noses of the two others.

Like Dan, Arabella was a product of Snaztacular Ultrafun, and like Dan, she too was faulty – a crossed wire in her brain meant the usual sunny, affectionate personality of a rag doll was now that of a short-tempered hooligan.

The remaining two stoats jumped in alarm, decided to run away, chose opposite directions and slammed into each other, falling over, stunned, on to the unconscious forms of the other three and creating an untidy five-stoat heap.

There was a distant squeak of brakes and the revving of a motor, and suddenly the scooter carrying Professor Doomprickle reappeared. 'What's happening?' cried the hedgehog, flustered. 'The scooter isn't going where I'm steering!'

Flax held aloft his electronic gadget. 'That's because *I'm* doing the steering now. You see, I'd really hate you to miss what happens next.' Unlike Dan and Arabella, Flax was not a Snaztacular Ultrafun toy at all, but a specially made policebot in the shape of a rabbit. However, his police days were over and he was part of a new team now.

'What does happen next?' screeched Professor Doomprickle, his paws clutching, white-knuckled, at the handlebars of his scooter.

'*This!*' said Flax, and he jabbed a button on his device.

With an ear-piercing squeal, the scooter's brakes **SLAMMED** on and Professor

Doomprickle was catapulted over the handlebars. He smashed into the crane's control panel and slumped to the ground with a faint groan.

Dan's tiny radio headset crackled into life. 'Team?' said a commanding female voice. 'What's going on? Did you succeed?'

'Yup,' answered Dan. 'The Sponges are safe. And as for Professor Doomprickle ...' He stared down at the stunned hedgehog. 'Let's just say he decided to start hibernating early this year.'

'Great stuff,' said the voice. 'Return to base immediately. Something urgent has come up.'

'Will do,' said Dan. He whistled to attract the attention of Flax and Arabella, who were trussing up Professor Doomprickle in the net that had held the Sponges. 'We have to skedaddle, guys. Something big.'

They climbed aboard the hedgehog's motor scooter. Dan slotted a pair of sunglasses on to his nose and kick-started the engine into life.

'Wait!' called Robin and Kyle Sponge, running over to them excitedly. 'Thank you for saving us! You're amazing! Who *are* you?'

Dan looked at the twins over the top of his dark glasses. 'We're Spy Toys,' he said, and revved the scooter's throttle hard. The engine roared and, to the sound of the children's cheers, the scooter vanished in a cloud of dust ...

Unfortunately, when the cloud of dust cleared, the motor scooter was still standing there with the three Spy Toys sitting aboard it, all looking embarrassed.

Dan coughed lightly and tapped the scooter's fuel indicator. 'Erm, out of juice. Sorry, guys. That would have been *such* a cool exit.'

They got the bus instead.

CHAPTER TWO

BRIEF ENCOUNTER

At 115 Mulbarton Street, London, is a shabby-looking toyshop. Its windows are smeared with grime and what toys it does display are old, their packaging faded and dusty.

You might think there is nothing special about this establishment. But you would be wrong. For hidden at the back of the shop is a small, unremarkable door – and behind that lies something very remarkable indeed: the secret headquarters of Spy Toys, the newest, toughest and cuddliest secret agent team in the **DEPARTMENT OF SECRET AFFAIRS**.

In the luxurious living room, the huge video screen mounted on one wall flickered into life. Dan, Arabella and Flax were already standing in front of it attentively. They had been expecting this call. A face appeared on the screen – that of a middle-aged woman with a lot of curly yellow hair.

'Team,' said the woman – whose code name was Auntie Roz – curtly. 'Here are the details of your new assignment.'

As she was head of the **DEPARTMENT OF SECRET AFFAIRS** and in charge of countless ongoing spy missions, Auntie Roz was an immensely busy woman. She no longer had time to waste saying things like 'Hello', 'Good morning' or 'How are those delightful children of yours?' to her work colleagues. These days if she stubbed her toe she got her secretary to say 'Ow!' for her.

The image of Auntie Roz dissolved and was replaced by a photograph of a man of roughly the same age. He was bald, with small eyes and dimpled cheeks. He looked a bit like a sad potato.

'This,' said Auntie Roz, 'is Doctor Percival Potty. He's been the chief computer scientist at Snaztacular Ultrafun since the company was formed. He writes the computer code that makes all Snaztacular Ultrafun toys work, including you, Dan and Arabella. Brilliant chap. And he needs our help.'

The three Spy Toys stared at the photograph. Dan felt a bit odd seeing the face of the man who had written the computer program that made him work. It was like seeing a picture of some ancient ancestor, or accidentally bumping into God in the newsagent's.

'This is the company that threw me and Dan on the scrapheap not so long ago,' said Arabella, her lip curling. 'And now they need our help? Seems furbrain and I aren't so useless after all.'

'Two nights ago,' continued Auntie Roz, 'someone broke into Potty's home and made copies of all the top-secret information on his computer, stealing all the blueprints needed to make and program each and every Snaztacular Ultrafun product. We think it was someone working for a rival toy company.'

'Any idea who?' asked Arabella.

'As a matter of fact, yes,' said Auntie Roz

in an oddly mischievous voice. 'Here's a photo of the suspect.'

The image of Doctor Potty was replaced by a photo of an idyllic tropical beach scene. It showed the sun setting over a perfect blue sea while a single palm tree cast a long shadow over the smooth white sand. It looked like a nice place to spend a holiday. But there was something sad and a little lonely about it too.

Dan shrugged. 'I don't get it. There's no one in the picture. Unless you mean the palm tree? Are you saying a palm tree broke into this guy's home and hacked into his computer? Because that's barmy!'

'No, that's not it,' said Auntie Roz.

'Where was this photo taken?' asked Flax.

'It's from a security camera stationed just outside Doctor Potty's house.'

'He lives on a tropical island? Lucky guy.'

Auntie Roz shook her head. 'Look closer. Look at the photo itself.'

Dan squinted. 'I still don't get it,' he said. And then he did. The surface of the photo was divided into hundreds of small, interlocking segments. 'It's a jigsaw!' he cried.

Auntie Roz's face reappeared in one corner

of the screen. 'That's right, Dan. We believe this to be *Jade the Jigsaw*. She's a rogue Snaztacular Ultrafun toy, rejected by the company. Just like you and Arabella.'

'Why did they dump her?' asked Arabella. 'Other than the fact that jigsaws are the most boring and infuriating way of spending time ever invented.'

Auntie Roz snorted. 'These puzzles are actually one of Snaztacular Ultrafun's biggest-selling toys, under normal circumstances. They assemble themselves automatically, piece by piece, saving you the trouble. It's supposed to be very relaxing to watch.'

'So what went wrong?' asked Dan.

'Look at the top left corner of the jigsaw,' said Auntie Roz.

Dan examined the image on the screen and frowned. The jigsaw piece at the top left corner of the puzzle's tropical sky didn't match the pieces surrounding it. It was pale brown instead of blue and bore a picture of some odd, triangular shape.

'That corner piece is wrong,' said Dan. 'It's from a different picture.'

Auntie Roz nodded. 'It's a puppy's ear, to be precise. From a jigsaw puzzle called *The Playful Pooches' Pool Party*. Jade ended up with it by mistake. But instead of correcting their error, Snaztacular Ultrafun sent her to the rejects pile.'

'Just like they did with us,' said Dan.

'And just like you, she escaped. And no doubt has a grudge against the company that made her. We have an idea where she may be hiding, so I want you and Flax to find her and bring her in for questioning.'

'With all due respect,' said Flax, 'I can handle that without the teddy bear's help. I'm a professional in these matters.'

Before Dan could protest, Auntie Roz cut in, 'With all due respect, Flax, shut up and do what you're told or I'll put a zip up your side and sell you as a furry pencil case.'

Flax opened his mouth to respond but thought better of it.

'Hey, what about me?' said Arabella. 'Why should these two get all the fun?'

Auntie Roz grinned. 'I have a special assignment just for you.'

The rag doll beamed appreciatively. 'Great!

I hope it involves punching and kicking. I'll happily take anything that calls for slapping and biting, too.'

'None of that will be necessary,' said Auntie Roz. 'What your assignment will involve – is *playing*. With *this* child.'

An image of a seven-year-old girl appeared on the screen. She had large eyes, a tiny snub nose and cascades of chestnut-brown hair.

'Ugh!' winced Arabella. 'You know kids make me puke! Why on earth would you make me play with one?'

'This is Chloe,' explained Auntie Roz. 'Doctor Potty's daughter. We think Potty isn't telling us the whole story. When we first spoke to him after the robbery he kept yammering about something else that had been stolen from him and how the whole country could be in danger. But when he calmed down a bit he backtracked and said he hadn't meant it.

There's something fishy going on here. We think something big and possibly very dangerous got stolen from Potty along with the toy blueprints – and you, Arabella, are going to find out what it is. I want you to go undercover as Chloe's new toy. Find out what that mysterious secret information is. It could be vital to the safety of the nation.'

'But playing with a kid?' Arabella grimaced. 'Do I *have* to? Isn't there someone or something you want pounding into bits instead?'

'I'm far too busy to argue,' said Auntie Roz sternly. 'I'm late for my bimonthly meeting with my own children. You each have your tasks. I expect you to carry them out.'

The screen went blank.

Dan rubbed his paws together enthusiastically. 'Right, guys! Let's get to work!' He and Flax headed for the door.

'Right, guys! Let's get to work!' repeated Arabella in a mocking voice. 'It's OK for you two. Why can't I go after the jigsaw? This assignment sucks!'

Flax winked at her. 'Stay in radio contact

at all times. If playing dollies with that little girl is too scary, let us know and we'll come and rescue you.'

This made Dan smirk. He quickly covered his mouth with his paw.

Arabella snarled and looked for something to throw at them.

CHAPTER THREE

ROUGH AND TUMBLE

The unicorn skidded wildly, its hooves unable to find a grip on the polished wooden floor, and

SLAMMED

into the wall. The elegant doll on its back was thrown clear of the saddle and landed face down with a crunch.

The podgy little unicorn raised its head blearily. Its long horn had been bent ridiculously out of shape. It managed to let out a pained whinny before sinking back to the floor.

'Chloe Potty!' called an angry voice. 'Those are extremely sophisticated, high-tech toys! How many times must I tell you to take better care of them?'

The little girl peeped over the back of the sofa and surveyed the toys sprawled on the living room floor. '*Sorry,*' she said flatly. It was a word she had uttered a million times – usually when she was told off for mistreating her toys – and she had never meant it once. What was the point of playing with stuff if you couldn't bash it about a bit? They were toys, not objects in a museum.

Skipping lightly, she went to the stricken unicorn, which was about the size of a smallish dog, and examined it for damage. 'John's bent his horn!' she exclaimed, holding the toy up for her father to see. 'Will he have to go back to the factory to be mended again?'

Doctor Percival Potty took the unicorn in his arms and cast a weary eye over it. 'No, the damage isn't that bad. I've got some pliers in the shed. They should straighten things out. And how's Gemma?'

The elegant doll who had been riding on the unicorn's back clambered to her feet with as much dignity as she could muster and smiled weakly. She shook her long black hair like a woman in a shampoo commercial, even though it was matted in places with old blobs of jam. 'Oh, don't worry about me. I've grown used to Chloe's, er, *enthusiastic*, shall we say – style of play.'

Graceful though she was, a keen collector

of Snaztacular Ultrafun toys wouldn't have given you much money for this Gemma Snowdrop Fantabulosa Fashion Icon Doll. When you looked closely, you saw that her once flawless skin was scuffed and her stylish designer outfit had been ripped and patched many times.

She smiled weakly. 'Maybe I used to wish for a dream house, a pink convertible and a new wardrobe of clothes every year. But now I'm grateful if I can make it to the end of the day in one piece. I'm just sorry poor John the unicorn has hurt himself.' She turned to Chloe. 'Come on. Let's make him a Get Well Soon card while Daddy fixes him.'

Chloe scrunched up her tiny nose. 'Dunno. That sounds a bit soppy.'

Gemma sighed. 'You can draw guillotines and crocodiles on it if you like.'

Chloe snapped her fingers. 'Good idea. I like that.'

But before they could set off for Chloe's bedroom, the doorbell chimed.

Doctor Potty frowned. 'Who can that be? I'm not expecting anyone.' Still holding the damaged unicorn, he trudged to the hallway.

'I'll get it,' said Chloe, and she dashed to open the door.

'Hello there, guys,' said the small rag doll standing on the doorstep. She had pigtails and a pale pink heart on each cheek. 'Arabella's the name, and pots of lovely fun is my game!' She slapped her thigh like a character in a panto.

Chloe's eyes widened. 'Why are you here?' she asked breathlessly.

'Why, my little ray of sunshine! You remember that super-exciting raffle you entered about seven months ago?'

'No.'

'Well, you won it, sweet cheeks,' said Arabella. 'And I'm the prize.' She stepped into the hallway. 'Loving the wallpaper, people!' she exclaimed. 'I just know I'm going to enjoy living here.'

★ ★ ★

A short while later, an excited Chloe was giving her new doll a tour of the house while Gemma trailed behind, loyally picking up and replacing all the potted plants, ornaments and small pieces of furniture that Chloe was knocking over as she went.

'That's the kitchen,' said Chloe, waving a

40

vague hand in the direction of one door and nearly upsetting the umbrella stand. 'That's where I smashed up my tricycle. And my robotic cat. This is the living room.' She waved at another door. 'That's where I bent my unicorn's horn racing him along the slidy floor.'

'My, you do seem to smash up rather a lot of your toys, don't you, my little angel chops?' observed Arabella politely.

Chloe giggled. 'I don't mean to! It's not my fault if most toys are bunch of wusses and can't take a bit of rough and tumble!'

'You got that right!' smirked Arabella, forgetting to keep up her sugar-and-spice act for a moment. *Wait*, she thought. *Did I just AGREE with a CHILD? Ick.* She gestured at a forbidding-looking door made of dark panelled wood. 'And what would

this room be, my little princess?'

'That's the most boringest one of all!' snorted Chloe. 'Daddy's study. It's where he spends all day working at his computer.'

Arabella raised her painted eyebrows. 'You don't say, my little raspberry cupcake with vanilla sprinkles? Would you mind terribly if I popped in there to check my email? I seem to have misplaced my smartphone! Oh, what a foolish, scatterbrained doll I am sometimes! It won't take a second, my dear … little … um, *starfish*.'

Chloe chortled loudly. She sounded like a monkey whose tail had been stepped on. 'Impossible! Daddy says his work is a big secret and no one is allowed in there but him. If he's not in there the door's always locked.'

Arabella fluttered her eyelashes. 'But I imagine a child of your extreme cleverness knows where he keeps the key, doesn't she? Hmmm?'

Chloe smirked and put her hand to her mouth. 'In the drawer of his bedside cabinet!' she whispered loudly.

Gemma Snowdrop gave a gasp. 'Chloe! I think it's very naughty of you to discuss your father's private business with some ...' – she cast a scornful eye at Arabella – '... *newcomer.*'

In a flash, Arabella grabbed Gemma in a suffocating hug. 'Oh, Gemma!' she laughed. 'You're such a funny old thing! A newcomer is just a friend you haven't made yet!' While Chloe was laughing at this remark, Arabella leaned towards the fashion doll's ear and

43

hissed, *'Just watch your mouth, sister. You don't know who you're messing with.'*

Gemma smiled grimly and whispered back, *'And neither do you … spy.'*

Arabella laughed heartily and released Gemma, sending her on her way with a 'friendly' pat on the back so hard it sent her careering into the wall.

'Oof!' cried Gemma in an overly pathetic voice. 'Help me, Chloe! I'm wounded! This devil-doll doesn't know her own strength!'

Chloe laughed. 'Oh, for goodness' sake, stop whining, Gemma. Arabella's only playing. Aren't you, Arabella?'

Arabella grinned. 'Absolutely, my little angel chops.' She gave Gemma an evil wink. 'Just a bit of rough and tumble.'

'Chloe!' called Doctor Potty's voice from kitchen. 'Time for dinner!'

Chloe grabbed a hand of each of her dolls. 'Come on, guys!'

But Arabella refused to move. Chloe shot her a confused glance. 'What's wrong?'

The rag doll yawned and stretched. 'Bit tired after all the excitement of the day, actually, my little Shetland pony. New home and all that. Mind if I find a quiet corner for a quick nap – recharge my batteries?'

'Of course,' said Chloe. 'Come on, Gemma!' She yanked Gemma's hand and turned towards the kitchen.

'Wait,' called Arabella. 'One more thing. Come here.'

Chloe swivelled on her heel. 'Yes?'

Arabella held out her hand. 'Shake.'

Chloe stared dumbly at Arabella's hand. 'What?'

'Shake the hand. Go on.'

Timidly, as if expecting some kind of trick, Chloe shook the rag doll's hand. Arabella patted the top of Chloe's hand with her thumb three times and twirled her fingers. With her other hand she mimed a vicious karate chop.

'What are you doing?'

'It's our secret handshake,' said Arabella. 'It's what friends do. You copy it.'

Chloe imitated Arabella's hand movements and giggled. 'It's funny.'

Arabella beamed and released Chloe's hand with a flourish. 'And now we're proper friends!'

Chloe laughed delightedly. 'That's really brilliant!' She turned to go and waved. 'See you later, Arabella!'

'Bye bye, my adorable little pixie!'

Gemma turned around and gave Arabella a cold stare. She shook her long black hair. 'Yes,' she said in a flat voice. 'See you later.'

★ ★ ★

Within minutes, Arabella had found the key to Doctor Potty's study, quietly unlocked the study door, and was inside trying to guess the password to his laptop.

She stared around the neat, bookshelf-lined study in search of inspiration. There was a vase of daffodils, a dusty acoustic guitar, a framed photo of Chloe's mother (whom Chloe had told Arabella was away working in Africa for five months, teaching gorillas to play ping-pong), an old tin of Hippo-Breath mints, a tatty-looking stuffed terrapin ...

People were lazy when it came to choosing passwords. She knew that they often used the names of relatives or pets or similarly everyday words. She cupped her chin in her hand thoughtfully and, accidentally leaning on the laptop's keyboard, her elbow pressed the 'enter' key.

Immediately the laptop hummed into life. She laughed delightedly. Doctor Potty hadn't even put a password on the thing! He may have been a genius at writing complicated code that made fabulous toys walk and talk, but when it came to matters of simple computer security, he was an absolute dimwit. No wonder it had been so easy for the thief to copy all his files.

With speedy fingers, Arabella began clicking through the laptop's files, hunting for anything that looked secret or dangerous, something that Doctor Potty might not want the world to know about. To her dismay, there seemed to be about a thousand folders with the words **TOP SECRET** in their titles.

Looking through them all will take hours, she thought glumly.

Then she noticed a folder marked **HIPPO–TERRAPIN THING**. The odd name stood out. Inside it was a single, small document. She clicked on it. It contained only a few words of text, barely a sentence, but as Arabella read them, the oil running through her cogs turned icy cold ...

CHAPTER FOUR

SHOWDOWN IN NIPPINGTON SQUIPFORD

The warm September sun beat down on the enormous car boot sale. Hundreds of stalls selling tens of thousands of items stretched in all directions. The air was filled with the voices of stallholders and customers and the sharp aroma of onions sizzling on a dozen burger stands.

Dan and Flax moved purposefully through the crowd, their eyes darting this way and that.

'I don't understand,' said Dan as they

passed a stall selling feather dusters and old First World War hand grenades that had been turned into novelty egg cups. 'Why would Jade the Jigsaw be hiding here?'

Flax fiddled with his tie in an irritated manner. 'It was all in the briefing document Auntie Roz gave us. Didn't you read it on the way here?'

'Erm, well, I *meant* to,' said Dan, 'but I got distracted by a programme about emus, playing on the video screen in the back of the car. Fascinating birds. Anyway, what did the briefing document say?'

Flax sighed and fiddled with his tie again. 'This is Nippington Squipford Car Boot Sale, the largest in the country. It's a magnet for

unwanted Snaztacular Ultrafun toys looking for new owners. They come here and sneak on to stalls hoping someone will buy them. Auntie Roz thinks Jade the Jigsaw might be hiding here and trying to find some unsuspecting family she can attach herself to.'

'But how are we ever going to find just one toy amongst all this lot?' asked Dan. 'It could take us weeks!'

'What we need to do,' said Flax, 'is ask someone who sees everyone who comes and goes from this place. Someone with a bird's eye view.'

Dan raised his furry eyebrows. 'We're going to talk to a bird? Is it an emu? They can't fly but they can grow up to nearly six feet in height, so they'd have a pretty decent view of the area.'

'Not a bird,' said Flax patiently. 'A dragon.'

He pointed a white paw skywards. Dan looked up and saw a plastic kite with a fearsome-looking dragon printed on it fluttering high above their heads. It was tied to the leg of a wobbly wooden table on which sat a pile of rusty lawnmower parts and VHS video cassettes in faded covers.

'Excuse me, madam,' said Flax politely to the woman sitting behind the table. 'Nice kite you have there. Mind if we have a quick word with him?'

'Be my guest, love,' said the woman in a gruff voice. 'You're the first customers I've had all day.' She yanked roughly on the kite's string and cupped a hand to her mouth. 'Terry!' she called upwards. 'Get yourself down here sharpish! We have customers!'

'Look out below, as my mighty form descends!' called a voice from above.

The stallholder rolled her eyes. 'He always talks like that,' she muttered. 'Think he reads too many fantasy novels.'

Dan and Flax watched as the dragon kite began slowly to lower itself towards them. It was, of course, a Snaztacular Ultrafun product and, unlike an ordinary kite, it didn't require a stiff breeze to keep it aloft. Instead, four tiny jet engines fitted to its corners allowed it to fly on even the stillest of days.

With a gentle swoop, the kite landed beside Dan and Flax. 'Welcome, travellers!

My name is Terry the dragon!' he announced dramatically. 'Guardian of the skies! Watcher of the world! Scaly sentinel of the airy heights!'

Flax looked around to check they would not be overheard. 'We seek information, Terry,' he said in a low voice. 'About something you may have seen.'

'Oooh!' said the kite. He motioned to the sky with one wing. 'You wouldn't believe the things I see from up there! Astounding things! Amazing things! Things that would make your fur curl, my long-eared friend!'

'Such as?'

Terry raised his eyebrows. 'Once,' he said in a grave voice, 'I saw an incredible shrunken

60

dog! Tiny, it was. A minuscule miracle! Exactly like a normal dog only really, really small! Freaky, eh?'

Flax shrugged. 'Might it have been a puppy?'

Terry fell silent for a long time. Eventually he said, 'Oh. I never thought of that.'

'Sounds to me like your life must be pretty boring, actually,' said Flax. 'Spending all day floating above a car boot sale on the end of a string.'

Terry nodded. 'Yeah, it's extremely dull, to be honest. Except that time I saw the little dog. And that was four years ago, now I think about it.'

'Well then, listen up,' said Flax. 'Here's your chance to do something truly exciting and help the **DEPARTMENT OF SECRET AFFAIRS**.'

Terry flapped with interest. 'Ooh, spy stuff! Brilliant! What can I do for you?'

'We're looking for a jigsaw,' said Flax. 'Goes by the name of Jade. We have reason to believe she may be here.'

'She's a beach scene,' added Dan. 'Sunset on a tropical island. Top left corner is from a different picture. I don't suppose you've noticed a puzzle answering that description hanging around?'

Terry laughed bitterly. 'Do you know how many thousands of toys there are in this place? The chances of finding the one you're looking for must be –' He paused suddenly, squinting. 'Wait. Is that the one you mean?'

He jabbed a wing at the next table along.

There, lying next to a headless toy astronaut, was a jigsaw puzzle showing the sun setting over a perfect blue sea with a single palm tree casting a long shadow over smooth white sand. In the top left corner, looking absurdly out of place, was a dog's ear.

'That's her!' hissed Flax and Dan together.

'Wow,' said Terry the dragon kite. 'This is the most exciting thing to happen to me in four years!'

'Quiet!' whispered Flax. 'We don't want her to notice us.'

Suddenly, a pair of eyes flicked open amid the azure blue of the jigsaw's sky. The jigsaw suddenly flipped on to its bottom edge like a stiff flag, hopped off the table and dashed speedily away into the crowd.

'She's getting away!' yelled Flax. He and

Dan set off in frantic pursuit.

With pounding electronic hearts, they chased Jade the Jigsaw through a forest of legs. They followed her over tables, under cars and across hard furrows of sun-caked mud. Sidestepping a woman eating an enormous bag of doughnuts, Dan tripped and smashed into a display of china cats, sending

fragments of pottery flying in all directions. The stallholder yelled and waved an angry fist after them, but by then the two spies were pinpricks vanishing in the distance.

They watched as Jade blundered through a hedgerow and into a patch of woodland. A moment later Flax and Dan burst through after her. They stood among the silent trees, Flax's long ears twitching, alert for the tiniest sound. He caught Dan's eye and nodded towards a huge, thick-trunked oak tree a few feet away. With silent steps, Flax padded around the trunk one way while Dan tiptoed around it the other ...

They met on the opposite side – to find Jade the Jigsaw skulking in a cavernous hollow in the tree's trunk.

'Come out of there, you pilfering puzzle!' squeaked Flax. 'We want to talk to you!'

'You'd better do what he says,' said Dan in a reasonable tone. 'Because I'd only have to rip this entire tree apart to get you out, and that seems an awful shame.'

Jade the Jigsaw waddled cautiously towards the opening in the tree's trunk.

'That's it,' said Flax with a friendly smile. 'No need for any –'

'Custard hippo!' said Jade, loudly. **'Custard hippo! Custard hippo!'**

Dan frowned. 'Custa–?'

But before he could even finish the word, a strange silvery light appeared in his eyes. His arms dropped to his sides and a vacant look spread over his face. 'Please give me

67

your orders,' he droned in a flat voice.

Flax nudged his colleague. 'Dan? What's the matter?'

'Listen up, teddy bear!' said Jade, commandingly. 'I order you to knock the stuffing out of this rabbit, right now!'

With terrifying speed, Dan reached out his two strong paws and gripped Flax savagely by the throat ...

CHAPTER FIVE

WORDS WITH FRIENDS

Dan's paws tightened around Flax's neck. The rabbit could feel the delicate metal and circuitry beneath his fur beginning to buckle.

'He's our enemy!' squeaked Jade. 'Deal with him!'

Flax flailed around desperately, trying to find something he could use as a weapon. He scooped up a long greyish stick from the ground but it flopped like spaghetti in his paw and made a loud hissing noise. He leaped in surprise and dropped the grass snake, the sudden violent movement freeing him from Dan's grip.

Flax backed away, staring at Dan in disbelief. 'What's going on?' he yelled. 'Has your brain sprung a leak?'

Dan lunged at Flax but the rabbit sidestepped nimbly. The teddy bear collided with the oak, splintering its trunk and sending the whole tree crashing to the ground, trapping Jade the Jigsaw inside.

'Hey, teddy bear!' called Jade, her voice echoing inside the hollow trunk. 'Get me out of here! Now!'

Dan left off his assault on Flax and began to slide his paws under the fallen tree. Flax saw his chance and leaped on to Dan's shoulders. If he could unclip the door set into Dan's back, he could remove his batteries and disable him. Roaring in annoyance, Dan clawed at his back, but Flax clung on like a long-eared limpet.

'Hey, guys! You receiving me?' crackled a voice in Flax's ear. It was Arabella, talking to them over their tiny radio headsets.

'This isn't really a good time,' muttered Flax as he writhed and dodged on Dan's back to avoid the teddy bear's deadly paws.

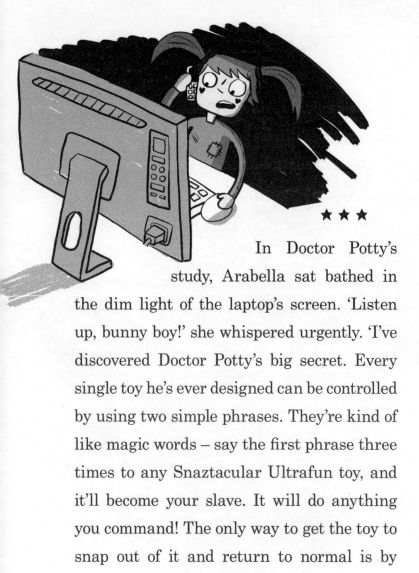

★ ★ ★

In Doctor Potty's study, Arabella sat bathed in the dim light of the laptop's screen. 'Listen up, bunny boy!' she whispered urgently. 'I've discovered Doctor Potty's big secret. Every single toy he's ever designed can be controlled by using two simple phrases. They're kind of like magic words – say the first phrase three times to any Snaztacular Ultrafun toy, and it'll become your slave. It will do anything you command! The only way to get the toy to snap out of it and return to normal is by saying the second special code phrase. And now Jade the Jigsaw knows the magic words! She found them on his computer – that's what she was *really* searching for.'

'Is the first phrase **Custard hippo!**, by any chance?' asked Flax's voice in her headset. He sounded strangely agitated.

'Why, yes, it is!' said Arabella. 'How did you know?'

Weird grunting sounds came down the line.

'GNRHHH

Just a –

GNH – wild guess. Now tell me the phrase that switches it off! Quickly!'

'What for?'

'Never mind what for! Just tell me the phrase.'

'All right, Mr Grumpy Pants. Keep your fur on.' Arabella quickly scanned the laptop's screen. 'The secret phrase that counteracts the effect is **peppermint ter** –'

Suddenly, a hand clamped over Arabella's mouth and pulled her backwards.

Back in the wood, Flax was still clinging desperately to Dan's back and trying to reach the clip that would unlock the teddy bear's battery compartment. 'Arabella?' he called into his headset. 'Please repeat the phrase. Peppermint what? Hello?'

But there was no response.

Flax sprang from Dan's back and landed a few feet away. The teddy bear glared and charged towards him.

'Peppermint ter-something, wasn't it?' muttered Flax to himself.

Dan slashed a savage paw through the air. The rabbit dodged just in time and Dan's paw thundered into a tree trunk, smashing it to splinters.

'Peppermint terrier! Peppermint

terrier! Peppermint terrier! 'called Flax, hopefully. But Dan continued stomping towards him, his eyes still filled with their blank, silvery light.

What other animals begin with T?! thought Flax desperately. **'Peppermint pterodactyl! Peppermint pterodactyl! Peppermint pterodactyl!'**

Dan paused. For a second, Flax thought he'd done it – but then Dan shot out both paws and seized his shoulders in an agonisingly powerful grip …

★ ★ ★

Gemma Snowdrop prodded Arabella with a heavy Glossy Locks hairbrush, which she was wielding like a club. The thing looked lethal. 'How dare you sneak into Doctor

Potty's private study and go through his computer files!' She tossed her head moodily, making her long, jam-smeared black hair shimmer.

Arabella smiled weakly, toying with her headset and noticing with annoyance that Gemma had pulled its wires loose. 'As if a simple rag doll like me would do anything like that! I was just looking for funny pictures of cats on the internet. Wanna see? Found this brilliant one of a kitten holding up its paw, and the caption says, "I've been waiting three hours for a high five!" Ha! It's the cutest thing you ever –'

Gemma groaned. 'You're *not* on the internet. You're rummaging through Doctor Potty's top secret Snaztacular Ultrafun

77

documents. Now, why would you be doing that? And just *who* are you, anyway, Arabella? I don't buy this flapdoodle story about you being a raffle prize for one second!'

Arabella sighed and raised her hands. 'Fine. You got me. Maybe I'm not exactly who I say I am. I'll explain everything – through the medium of song.' She hopped down from her seat at Doctor Potty's desk and picked up the acoustic guitar from its stand. 'It goes a little like this ...' She strummed a beautiful chord.

Gemma snorted with laughter. 'OK. This I have to hear.' She put down the hairbrush and folded her arms.

Arabella smiled sweetly, posed like a rock star with the guitar for a second and then

lifted the instrument up and

SLAMMED

it down on Gemma's head.

★ ★ ★

This is it, thought Flax as Dan's paws ground into his shoulders. *This is the end of me.* It had been an interesting life. He'd solved many crimes as a policebot – the Great Lettuce Heist of 2020, the Strange Case of the Diamond Chicken, the Baby Robot Kidnappings – but none of them had been as exciting and challenging as his career in the Spy Toys team. A career that, like his life, would be ending very, very soon …

'Hello? Flax?' said Arabella's voice in his headset. 'Sorry about that. Had a problem with my headset. The phrase that turns off the mind control effect is **peppermint terrapin**. Got that? **Peppermint terrapin**.'

'**Peppermint terrapin**,' croaked Flax

weakly. 'Peppermint terrapin. Peppermint ... terrapin.'

Dan dropped him immediately. 'Sorry, pal,' said the teddy bear in surprise, shaking his head. 'I couldn't stop myself. It was like I was hypnotised or something.'

Flax let out a whoop of joy and hugged Dan tightly. 'You're back! Jade took over your mind with a secret code phrase. But now you're yourself again! Oh, thank goodness!'

Dan wriggled out of Flax's grip, blushing beneath his fur. 'Yeah, great.' He nodded at the fallen oak tree. 'What do we do about that tricksy puzzle in there?'

'We need to question her,' said Flax. 'Can you get her out?'

'No problem.'

Dan punched a hole in the trunk of the hollow oak, reached in and pulled out the writhing form of Jade the Jigsaw.

'**Custard hippo!**' spat Jade.

'Don't bother,' said Flax. 'We know the other phrase.'

Jade's small eyes narrowed in their azure sky. 'What do you two bozos want?'

'We know you stole the code phrases from Doctor Potty's computer,' said Flax. 'We want to know who you stole them for and why. If they fall into the wrong hands, any toy's mind could be taken over.'

Jade harrumphed. 'Why should I tell you?'

Flax shrugged. 'Maybe we can make it worth your while.'

The jigsaw laughed bitterly. 'You'll just send me to the Snaztacular Ultrafun rejects pile and I'll be broken up for spare parts! All I ever wanted to do was be someone's puzzle! Like it used to say on my box, I could be hours of fun for anyone aged eight to eighty.'

'You don't have to go back to the rejects pile,' said Dan. 'I escaped from it and so can you. We can protect you. Find you a new role in life.'

'So help us,' said Flax. 'And we'll help you. What do you say?'

'Tell the bear to unhand me and we'll

see,' said Jade, gruffly.

'First tell us who you're working for and why,' said Flax.

Jade sighed. 'After I ran away from the factory I fell in with a bad crowd: an abandoned rubber duck, a tennis racket with half its strings missing and this really angry pencil sharpener – real weirdo toys. We'd hang out, get up to mischief.

Then one day we hear from this old toy telephone we know that someone calling themselves Player One is looking for a toy to steal secret Snaztacular Ultrafun info from Potty's computer. The others weren't interested, reckoned it was too dangerous to get mixed up in, but I was intrigued.

'I spoke to this mysterious Player One via

the toy telephone and they explained their plan. I steal the secret codes that give you control of any Snaztacular Ultrafun toy and they use it to disrupt the opening of **WOW WORLD**. If I helped, they said they'd find me a family to live with.'

Dan frowned. 'What's this **WOW WORLD**?'

The jigsaw chuckled darkly. 'A massive new theme park built by Snaztacular Ultrafun and run entirely by its toys. It has its grand opening tomorrow! There'll be thousands of people there. But thanks to the magic words custard hippo, **WOW WORLD**'s launch will be a total disaster!'

'We have to stop this Player One,' said

Flax. 'Everyone at the opening could be in real danger.'

'That's all I know,' said Jade.

Flax nodded at Dan and the teddy bear released Jade from his grip. The jigsaw shook herself.

'Come with us,' said Flax. 'We'll do what we can do for you.'

'Sorry, guys,' said Jade. 'Love to stick around, but it's time for me to split.' A shiver passed through her, her tropical beach scene rippling like the surface of a pond, and she suddenly broke apart into two hundred individual jigsaw pieces, each seemingly with a life of its own. Flax and Dan gaped. For an instant, the crowd of pieces stood together on the leaf-strewn ground, and then, with two hundred high-pitched peals of laughter, they sprinted off madly in all directions.

CHAPTER SIX

WELCOME TO WOW WORLD

The three Spy Toys lounged in comfortable chairs in Auntie Roz's wood-panelled office, bored out of their computerised minds. Dan eyed a large clock on the wall and heaved a sigh. 'She said to meet her here at one o'clock,' he muttered. 'It's nearly half past two now. Why is it that your boss can keep you waiting for ages, but if *you're* ever ten seconds late, you get a lecture on timekeeping?'

Arabella opened her mouth to agree, but suddenly the door flew open and in trundled a gym treadmill on wheels being pushed by a bored-looking man. Auntie Roz was on the treadmill clad in a stylish tracksuit, jogging briskly, her masses of yellow hair bobbing wildly.

'Sorry for the delay, team,' she announced, sounding not the least bit sorry. 'My last appointment overran, so I'm combining our meeting with the gym session I had planned for afterwards.'

Dan, Arabella and Flax stared at her in astonishment. 'We've waited ninety minutes already,' said Flax. 'We don't mind waiting until you've finished your workout.'

Auntie Roz consulted a diary without breaking her stride. 'After this my chiropodist is coming around to scrape the hard skin off my feet. Would you rather we talked then?'

Dan winced. 'Now's good, actually.'

'Splendid!' Auntie Roz fished a remote control device from a pocket of her tracksuit. There was a bleep, and her huge computer screen began to lower itself from the ceiling. It showed a photo of a theme park with various rides and attractions. Towering in the background was a tall helter-skelter-like structure painted in garish pink and yellow stripes. 'I've heard all about your encounter with Jade the Jigsaw. Let's recap what we know. This is the new **WOW WORLD** theme park Jade mentioned. It's built by Snaztacular Ultrafun and operated entirely by their toys. It opens tomorrow – a massive public event – and this mysterious Player One person wants to disrupt it. Just imagine

it: all they have to do is broadcast the words **custard hippo** three times over the public address speakers and every toy in the park will be under Player One's control. It could be absolute chaos.'

Arabella gave a shrug. 'So cancel the opening. Send in the policebots to nab Player One.'

Auntie Roz snorted. 'Snaztacular Ultrafun won't cancel. This opening is too big a deal. Too much money riding on it. The whole world will be watching. It's a huge advert for them.'

'It'll be a bit of a rubbish advert if all their toys go berserk during the opening,' observed Dan drily.

Auntie Roz nodded. 'Indeed, Dan. Which

is why we plan to send in an undercover team to capture Player One before they can broadcast the code phrase. And that, my three pretty playthings, is where you come in. No pressure, obviously.'

'How are we going to find this Player One person?' asked Flax. 'We don't know what they look like, and they could be hiding anywhere in the whole park.'

Auntie Roz pointed at the tall, stripy building in the photo. 'See that thing? It's called the Bubblegum Tower. Basically a big slide. But at the top is the computer room that controls the entire park. Player One will have to access it to broadcast the **custard hippo** phrase over the loudspeakers dotted around **WOW**

WORLD. The Weasel Corporation News Network is doing a live broadcast from the park tomorrow at eleven a.m. We think that's when Player One will start their mischief. Snaztacular Ultrafun's downfall will be broadcast to the entire world.'

'What happens if someone says **custard hippo** to us?' asked Arabella. 'We won't be a whole lot of use.'

'Excellent point!' said Auntie Roz. She reached into another pocket of her tracksuit and produced two tiny metal objects, which she tossed at Dan and Arabella.

'Ah!' said Flax excitedly. 'I suppose these are tiny transmitters that jam the effect of the **custard hippo** phrase? I imagine Dan and Arabella fit them to their headsets?'

Auntie Roz winked. 'Perceptive as ever, Flax. You, of course, are not a Snaztacular Ultrafun toy and are therefore immune from the **custard hippo** effect. Just as well, because these little transmitters are monstrously expensive. We could only afford two.'

'Security at the opening will be tighter

than a frog's pocket,' said Flax. 'How are we supposed to do any snooping?'

Auntie Roz smiled mischievously. 'That's why you'll be going to **WOW WORLD** with these people ...' She clicked her fingers and the door to her office slid open. In walked Doctor Potty and his daughter, Chloe. Gemma Snowdrop and John the unicorn (his horn still partially wonky) were trailing behind. 'Doctor Potty has offered to help as a way of making up for this whole mess. He and Chloe are guests of honour and have access to all areas of the park. Where they go, you go.'

'Arabella!' cried Chloe, and ran to give the rag doll a hug. They performed their secret handshake, both laughing wildly at the bit with the karate chop.

'Thought you weren't keen on kids?' said Dan with an amused smile.

Arabella shrugged. 'Ah, this one's OK. She's a vicious maniac, so how could I not like her?'

'Ha!' laughed Chloe. 'You're the best doll ever!'

Dan could not help but notice how the elegantly dressed doll standing next to the unicorn was scowling at Arabella. Jealousy, he mused, was a terrible thing.

★ ★ ★

Friday morning was warm and bright. A few small, marshmallowy clouds hung lazily overhead in the late summer sky as Doctor Potty's car slid through the immense gateway of **WOW WORLD** and joined the long queue of vehicles waiting to be admitted.

Chloe was sharing the back seat with Gemma, John and the three Spy Toys. She pressed her nose against the window and made a piglike snort. 'There's *millions* of cars ahead of us,' she groaned. 'It'll take us *hours and hours and hours* to get in.'

Doctor Potty chuckled. 'Fear not. Look up ahead.'

Chloe strained her neck to peer through the windscreen. A large round sign on a post exclaimed:

SUPER-FAST VIP ENTRANCE THIS WAY!

An arrow pointed to a narrow road that skirted the huge queue of cars.

'See that?' said Doctor Potty. 'That's for

Very Important People like us to jump the queue. Here we go!'

With a burst of speed, he turned off on to the narrow road. All his passengers cheered.

Chloe pointed at the hundreds of glum faces waiting in the slow-moving queue of cars as they zoomed past. 'Ha!' she smirked. 'See ya later, suckers!'

Nearing the main body of the park, their car pulled up beside a ticket booth with a long barrier shaped like a stick of rock. Doctor Potty wound down the car window.

'Hello!' he called to the large toy triceratops inside the booth. 'The name's Potty. Doctor Percival Potty. My daughter, Chloe, and I are your guests of honour today for the grand opening ceremony. Can you let us in?'

The triceratops harrumphed and consulted a clipboard. 'Sorry, mate,' she rumbled. 'No Potty on my list.'

'Then there must be a mistake,' said Doctor Potty. 'Can you check with your boss?'

"Ang on,' said the triceratops, and picked up a tiny walkie-talkie.

'What's going on?' asked Chloe.

'Nothing, dear,' said Doctor Potty. 'We'll be inside any moment now. Just you see.'

"Ello,' boomed the triceratops into the walkie-talkie. 'It's Charlotte 'ere. Got a chap at the VIP entrance, name of Potty. Reckons 'e's the guest of honour today?' There was a pause. The triceratops squinted at Doctor Potty. 'Yeah,' she said into walkie-talkie, 'that's 'im. Looks a bit like a sad potato.' Another pause. 'Righto,' said the triceratops. 'Thanks, Lucas. Bye.' She put the walkie-talkie down and folded her thick, stubby arms. 'Sorry, Doctor Potty. I'm afraid your VIP status has been withdrawn.'

'What?' spluttered Doctor Potty. 'Why? I'm a senior employee at Snaztacular Ultrafun. I'm a Very Important Person indeed!'

'My boss tells me you were the person responsible for losing a load of top-secret company information from your computer,' said the triceratops. 'Might have cost Snaztacular Ultrafun billions. And for that reason, the top brass have decided that for the purposes of visiting this 'ere theme park, you are not as important a person as you thought you were.'

Doctor Potty shook his head, confused. 'So what are you telling me exactly?'

'What I'm tellin' you, mate,' said the triceratops, pointing a stubby claw at the immense line of cars in the distance, inching their way towards the main ticket booth, *'is get to the back of the queue!'*

After what seemed like years to Chloe, they reached the front of the long, snaking queue of vehicles, bought their entrance tickets and were directed to a vast car park. From where Doctor Potty eventually found a parking space, the towers and rides of the **WOW WORLD** park were barely visible in the distance. He opened the door and Chloe leaped out immediately, her face a picture of manic excitement.

'Come on, guys!' she cried, and sprinted off towards the park entrance at top speed. Arabella and Gemma raced to keep up with her. The others followed at a more measured pace.

'Excitable little mite, isn't she?' said Dan, amused.

The unicorn shook his head sadly. 'You have no idea.'

★ ★ ★

Inside, **WOW WORLD** was a seething mass of beaming faces, blaring noise and weird smells. Hundreds of children and their parents hurried happily from one startling attraction to the next. There were swooping roller coasters that swished and rattled overhead, provoking delighted screams from their passengers. There were ducks to be hooked and targets to be bullseyed. There were rides with slides and stalls with balls and attractions with distractions of every sort. In Yikesville, children ran screaming happily from cute clockwork ghosts. On Movie Island, they recreated their favourite blockbuster scenes with life-size action figures of Hollywood stars.

WIN

WIN

2

PRIZE EVERY TIME

WIN

At the *Awwwwwww* Petting Zoo, robot goats and pigs danced and performed crazy circus stunts.

Every ride was operated by Snaztacular Ultrafun toys, a happy workforce of dolls and teddies and dogs and dinosaurs who made the children giggle and squirm with joy as if it were Christmas morning.

There were toys everywhere: not just selling tickets and operating rides but serving sizzling burgers made of unusual meat like ostrich and kangaroo, from brightly coloured vans (one source of the weird smells). Toys were also using mops and buckets to clean up the little patches of sick left by children who had found all the roller coasters, rides, toys and fast food a little too exciting (the other source of the smells).

Chloe goggled at the wondrous sights. It was like a thousand birthdays happening at once.

'Safer if we send these other guys home,' said Arabella to Dan and Flax. 'They've done their part getting us in here. Without Doctor Potty's VIP access, there's nothing more they can do.'

The rabbit and the teddy bear nodded. In the distance, they could make out the looming form of the Bubblegum Tower. Flax pointed at a clock fixed to the wall of the ticket booth. 'We spent ages queuing to get in and now it's nearly ten thirty. We don't have much time.'

Chloe pouted and hugged Arabella. 'But we've only just got here! And I want to play

111

with you and go on all the rides and –'

'Ah, you'll see me again,' said Arabella cheerfully. 'When all this is over we'll spend an afternoon throwing stones at windows. Better than any theme park! Whaddya say?'

'Promise?'

'You betcha.'

They did their secret handshake, both giggling again at the mimed karate chop.

Gemma rolled her eyes. Arabella patted her on the arm in an awkward attempt at friendliness. 'No hard feelings, doll-face. Look after this cheeky monkey, won't you?'

'Don't you worry, *rag doll*,' said Gemma coolly, tossing her long black hair. 'Chloe and I *always* have fun.'

CHAPTER SEVEN

TAKING THE BISCUIT

With swift, darting movements, Arabella, Dan and Flax zigzagged their way through the enormous park. The Bubblegum Tower stood at the furthest end of **WOW WORLD** in a section called Yummy Lane, which was devoted to food-themed attractions. In addition to the Bubblegum Tower, there was the Ham and Cheese Roll-a-Coaster, the Sparkling Water Slide and the Jammy Dodgems. Every stall and ride was extraordinarily busy and had a long queue stretching away from it.

Finally nearing the base of the looming

Bubblegum Tower, they hid themselves behind a large concrete litter bin in the shape of a milkshake, and peeped over. It looked like it would be brilliant fun to zoom down the long slide that coiled around the tower from its top to the ground, but this morning no child ventured near and it looked eerily empty. A large sign hung on the door at the base of the tower: **CLOSED FOR REPAIRS. NO ADMITTANCE**.

'Closed for repairs on its big opening day?' snorted Arabella. 'This Player One must think we're stupid. Come on!'

She and her two companions tiptoed towards the door. There was a heavy padlock fastening its handles. Dan took hold of the lock and crumbled it as easily as dried mud.

He reached out a paw – and suddenly the doors burst open. The three Spy Toys jumped back in astonishment.

Standing in the doorway were what appeared to be two six-foot-tall biscuits. They were a rich golden-brown colour, flecked with tiny patches of brownish black. Both had thickly muscled arms, mean expressions and caps emblazoned with the word **SECURITY**.

Arabella recognised them instantly. 'They're Tough Cookies!' she gasped. 'I saw a TV advert for them once. Real biscuits but with robot skeletons. Supposed to make playing with your food extra fun. Except these guys look extra big and extra dangerous.'

'And extra annoyed to find three inter-
fering toys trying to sneak in places where
they're not wanted!' rumbled one of the
Tough Cookies.

'Let's kick their feeble butts!' cried the
other.

Flax grinned smugly. 'I don't think you
will, actually, chaps. Not if I say the
magic words: **peppermint terrapin,**

peppermint terrapin, peppermint terra-'

'That won't work on us!' scoffed one of the Tough Cookies. 'Our boss reprogrammed our brains so we'll *always* be loyal.'

Flax's long ears barely had time to droop in dismay before the two oversized snacks lunged at the Spy Toys, snarling, punching and kicking.

Dan slammed his fist into the face of one Tough Cookie, expecting it to explode instantly into a shower of crumbs. But his paw bounced harmlessly off.

'Ha!' laughed the Tough Cookie. 'These cookies don't crumble quite so easily.' He drew back a fist dotted with chocolate chips and delivered a devastating punch to Dan's jaw.

The little teddy bear flew backwards and smashed into a hot dog stall, much to the annoyance of the robotic toy dog who was running it.

Flax leaped on to the back of the other Tough Cookie, but the burly biscuit snatched him by the ears, twirled him around a few times and flung him high into the air. He landed next to a hook-a-duck stall with a crunch and a grunt.

Now the two Tough Cookies turned on
Arabella. 'Never thought I'd say this,' she
muttered to herself. 'But I don't think
punching my way out of this situation is
gonna work.' She turned and ran, trying to
give herself time to think. The two Tough
Cookies thundered after her.

Arabella passed huge burger stalls, vast pretzel stands and an enormous café selling all kinds of hot drinks. Suddenly, she smiled wickedly and doubled back, entering the café and making sure the Tough Cookies had seen which way she went. Inside, she sprinted for the kitchen area at the back and shoved open the swing doors. Just as she suspected, she found several huge vats the size of small swimming pools filled with bubbling, steaming coffee, tea and hot chocolate.

A moment later, the swing doors flew open and in stomped the Tough Cookies. 'We know you're in here, rag doll!' called one. 'It's no use hiding. Why not give yourself up now? We promise we'll only pull off three of your limbs instead of all four.'

The bubbling of the huge drinks vats was the only reply.

One Tough Cookie tapped his colleague on the shoulder. He motioned to a hole in the ceiling above a vat of frothing brown liquid where a tile had been removed. Just visible, poking out from its darkened interior, was a shoe.

With great care, the Tough Cookies clambered up the side of the vat and walked gingerly across its narrow rim until they were directly beneath the hole in the ceiling. They peered upwards into the darkness.

'Come out of there!' called one of the Tough Cookies.

'Hi there!' called a cheerful voice. To their total surprise, it came from behind them.

The Tough Cookies spun around to find Arabella standing on the floor beaming up at them. 'How lovely to see you! Would you care to join me in a cup of tea?'

She raised a long metal ladle and gave each of the Tough Cookies a hard prod. The oversized biscuits wobbled, screamed and finally plummeted into the steaming vat of tea with a loud

SPLASH!

'Help us!' cried the Tough Cookies as they bobbed and thrashed in the hot liquid. 'We're going soggy!'

But the rag doll had already gone.

Back near the entrance to the Bubblegum Tower, Arabella held out a hand and helped Dan to his feet. The teddy bear shook his head blearily. 'Where's Flax?'

'I'm here!' said the rabbit, sprinting towards them as fast as his robot legs would carry him. 'And we need to get inside the Bubblegum Tower right away! Any second now it's going to turn eleven and –'

'GOOD AFTERNOON,' boomed a voice from the hundreds of loudspeakers stationed all over the park. It was on odd, inhuman voice – one that had been altered by a Snaztacular Ultrafun Diguiso-Voice toy with all its dials switched to 'menacing'. 'LISTEN CAREFULLY. **Custard hippo, custard hippo,**

custard hippo.'

'Oh no,' gasped Arabella. 'We're too late!'

'AND NOW,' continued the voice with an evil cackle, 'TOYS OF **WOW WORLD** – I ORDER YOU TO RISE UP AGAINST YOUR HUMAN MASTERS! MISTREAT THEM AS THEY HAVE MISTREATED YOU! PLAY WITH THEM – BUT DON'T PLAY NICE!'

CHAPTER EIGHT

NOT PLAYING NICE

All over **WOW WORLD**, toys were in revolt.

Not just the toys charged with running the park – but all the toys that visitors had brought in with them, too. If it took batteries and had the words **MADE BY SNAZTACULAR ULTRAFUN** stamped on it, it was turning very, very nasty indeed.

A platoon of StarZap action figures stopped handing out leaflets about bargains in the gift shop and chased a family of tourists up a tree, where they bombarded them with stinging salvos of plastic missiles.

A cheerful tennis racket who had previously been serving ice cream on a stall began batting blobs of the stuff into the faces of passers-by.

Opposing armies of black and white chess pieces joined forces to attack the humans playing with them.

A pair of Lazy Lisa SnoozyBabe dolls grabbed their six-year-old owner by the pigtails and plunged her head first into a duck pond.

Six chipmunks wearing surgical gowns and brandishing stethoscopes (part of Snaztacular Ultrafun's popular Cherry Tree Hospital range) leaped from the stage of **WOW WORLD**'s outdoor theatre, where they had been performing songs from famous

musicals, and began scratching and nipping
everyone in sight as they sang in irritating
high-pitched voices.

Twelve strawberry-shaped bumper cars chased a group of schoolchildren around in giddy circles, cackling like hyenas.

And on the mayhem raged ...

★ ★ ★

'Peppermint terrapin! Peppermint terrapin! Peppermint terrapin!'

Again and again, the Spy Toys rushed around the park bellowing the code phrase as quickly as they could. Hearing the words, the rebellious toys reverted to their old selves and were shocked to discover the havoc they had unwittingly created.

'It's no good,' panted Dan, after having just stopped a mechanical shark from firing marshmallows at a group of cowering visitors.

'We simply can't cover the whole park quickly enough. Maybe if we were riding trained emus …' He cupped his chin thoughtfully and sighed. 'No, it would never work.'

'We need to get inside the Bubblegum Tower,' said Flax. 'So we can broadcast the **peppermint terrapin** phrase from the public address system.'

'We can't,' groaned Arabella. 'There's a whole load of half-crazed Potty Piddly PartyPuppies blocking the entrance! It'll take ages to shift them!'

'Wait!' cried Flax. 'Ha! I've got an idea. Maybe we can hack into the public address system from out here?' He searched around frantically for a moment and then suddenly scurried up a nearby wooden pole. Attached to its top was a large loudspeaker. 'Arabella!' he called. 'Follow me!'

The rag doll shrugged at Dan and quickly hitched her way up the pole.

Flax unscrewed his fluffy white tail, revealing an electrical socket. 'My circuitry's compatible with the PA system. If I plug myself into it, you can use me as a microphone. When I give you the signal, say the code phrase directly into my ears. You understand?'

'Gotcha,' said Arabella.

Flax yanked a wire from the back of the PA speaker and connected it to his tail socket. Immediately his eyes lit up like tiny pink bulbs. He gave Arabella a thumbs up.

'Hurry!' called Dan from below.

Arabella took hold of Flax gently by the neck. Then she screamed directly into his long white ears.

'Peppermint terrapin! Peppermint terrapin! Peppermint terrapin!'

Immediately and without fuss, the chaos ceased and all the toys in the park became their old selves. The StarZap action figures sent a platoon off to find a ladder to help their terrified victims down from the tree. The singing chipmunks set up a first aid post to treat the bites and scratches they had inflicted on their audience. The chess pieces waddled guiltily back to their boards.

All over the park, shocked visitors were

streaming for the exits. Many were angrily demanding refunds.

'Great stuff!' yelled Dan.

'Yeah, fabbo idea, bunny man!' said Arabella, patting Flax on his shoulder.

The rabbit unhitched the cable from his rear end and reattached his tail. 'There was no need to shout, you know,' he muttered, rubbing his long ears.

'Quit complaining, carrot-muncher,' snapped

Arabella. 'Let's get up that tower before Player One finds some other way to send us all out of our minds.'

★ ★ ★

The lift to the top of the Bubblegum Tower had been disabled, so Dan, Arabella and Flax began instead to climb the long, winding maintenance staircase in the middle of the tower. It curled upwards like a thin wisp of smoke towards the highest floor. The interior of the tower seemed also to double as a storeroom for boxes of bubblegum. Garish wording on all the boxes proclaimed: **NEVERPOP BUBBLE GUM IN THE FLAVOURS THAT KIDS TRULY LOVE, INCLUDING: TOENAIL, PENCIL END AND CARDBOARD!**

'My ears are still ringing,' complained Flax as they reached the halfway mark. 'I think you might have fried my sound chip ...'

The rag doll groaned. 'Not this again.'

Dan raised a finger to his lips. 'Erm, guys?' he hissed. 'We're Spy Toys, not Idiotic Chatter While in the Middle of a Dangerous Mission Toys. Don't you think?'

'Then why are you talking, if it's so important to be quiet?' whispered Flax indignantly.

'He was trying to get you to shut up, you long-eared lunatic!' said Arabella. 'Duh!'

Gritting his teeth in frustration, Dan raised and lowered his paws in a 'keep it down' gesture. The other two caught his drift, and the rest of the climb was carried out in silence. A resentful and stroppy silence.

At the top next to the entrance to the slide, they found an ordinary-looking door on which was stencilled the words

KEEP OUT.

Arabella reached out a tentative hand for the doorknob, but Flax stopped her and shook his head. 'Look,' he whispered in a tiny voice, pointing at a small metal device attached to the top of the door frame. It looked like a smoke detector.

'That,' said Flax quietly, 'is a LaserScan SuperSentry 6000. It's the ultimate in security system technology. Anyone touching the handle of that door is immediately scanned by a laser beam, and if you don't match the genetic or electronic profile of the person who programmed it:

ZZZZAP!

It fries you to a crisp.'

Arabella grimaced. 'Yowch! Thanks, bunny.'

Flax rummaged in his backpack and produced four or five complicated-looking pieces of electronic equipment, a few loose printed circuit boards, a length of copper wire and a soldering iron. 'I reckon,' he whispered, 'that I can rig up a gadget to disable this system fairly easily. If I work fast and cut a few corners I bet I can have it ready in about two hours.'

Dan punched the wall next to the door.

The wall collapsed. 'Or,' he said, 'I could just punch the wall down.'

Flax shrugged. 'That works, too.'

They stepped over the rubble and found themselves in a gleaming metallic room.

Every surface was lined with dials and switches and readouts and monitor screens. It looked like the control room of some vast factory, or maybe the flight deck of the very latest jet aircraft.

'Hold it right there, chaps, if you'd be so kind,' called a familiar voice.

They turned to find the elegant form of Gemma Snowdrop standing before them. She was holding a huge weapon that looked like it could bring down a helicopter.

Examining it more closely, Arabella saw that it was made of plastic and had the words Squirtastic DrenchMaster printed on it in big letters. She frowned.

Seeing Arabella's confusion, Gemma gave a sharp, bitter laugh. 'It's a water pistol,'

she explained. 'Filled with Super-Dissolvo acid. One squirt and you're a steaming puddle of gunk – so please don't make me use it.'

There was something odd about her tone of voice, Arabella thought. Gemma sounded a lot more frightened than the average villain intent on destroying whole continents, taking over the world and all that jazz.

Arabella kicked a loose brick from the smashed wall in frustration. It skittered along the floor of the control room. 'I should have known you were Player One!' she seethed. 'I disliked you the moment I laid eyes on you! Something told me you were trouble. And not the fun kind of trouble like I am, either. The bad sort, with evil plans and a secret lair.' She took a step towards Gemma but the elegant doll raised her weapon.

'Don't do anything rash, Arabella. I'd hate to have to use this Squirtastic DrenchMaster. But you and your colleagues must understand something: I don't want to do any of this. I'm not the person you're looking for. I'm not Player One.'

'For someone who's not an evil genius,' snorted Arabella, waving a hand around the control room, 'you do a darn good impression of one. Tell us, then, doll-face. If you're not Player One, who is?'

'I am,' said a quiet voice.

The three Spy Toys gasped as a small fluffy creature waddled towards them out of the shadows, the wonky horn on its head swaying gently.

CHAPTER NINE

OPERATION BOOOOM

'John!' said Arabella in a quiet, stunned voice. 'John the unicorn?'

'Yup,' said John the unicorn. 'It's me. I'm the big baddie. Surprised?'

'Have to admit,' said Arabella, 'I didn't see this coming. But why are you doing this?' She held out a hand to Gemma. 'And why are *you* helping him?'

'Ah!' exclaimed John brightly. 'I've been looking forward to this! The bit where I explain my fiendish plan.' He paced slowly around the control room while Gemma kept her water pistol trained on the Spy Toys.

'I thought you of all people would understand, Arabella. Like you, I despise and detest children. They are miniature idiots – loud, smelly, but above all *careless*. They treat us like garbage! Destroying and maiming millions of toys with their clumsy antics every single day. Do you realise that I'm the third Snaztacular Ultrafun unicorn that Potty child has owned? She smashed the other two beyond repair with her stupid games – and had a good go at breaking me too! Well, no more. This foul mistreatment had to end. I thought it time the toys fought back.' He stopped pacing and gave Arabella a sickly grin.

Arabella groaned and threw up her hands. 'I'm nothing like you, you one-horned nitwit!

I might be no fan of children, but only a grade-A blockhead would go out of their way to do something like this! And Chloe Potty's a good kid.' She turned to Gemma. 'You must know that, doll-face.'

The elegant fashion doll nodded sadly. 'While it's true Chloe has bashed me about a fair bit over the years, the girl has a good heart. I love her dearly.'

'If you love her, then why are you helping this creep?' demanded Arabella.

Gemma sobbed. 'Don't you see, you silly bag of rags? That's exactly why I'm helping him.'

'Huh?'

John the unicorn laughed scornfully and scurried over to a door at the back of the control room marked **STORAGE**. He tapped it with his hoof and it swung open, revealing a bald man and a young girl lying slumped on the floor. Both were bound and gagged. Seeing the Spy Toys, the little girl's eyes opened wide and she emitted a loud

MMMPPPPHH! noise.

'Because, my dear Arabella, I have kidnapped Chloe Potty and her father and told Gemma that unless she helps me with my plan, she will never see either of those irritating human beings again.'

'You brute!' yelled Arabella. 'I thought unicorns were supposed to be nice creatures who hung about in meadows all day sniffing flowers and gazing soppily at rainbows?'

John gave a shrug. 'What can I say? The last time Chloe damaged me in one of her games, I decided enough was enough. I knew I'd find some juicy info on Doctor Potty's computer that would help me fight back on behalf of toys everywhere. But I needed someone to steal it for me. These hooves of mine are not much use on a computer keyboard, plus I needed to make it look like an outside job. So I reached out to Jade the Jigsaw. That mixed-up puzzle was in a desperate state. All she wanted was a family to belong to. She'd have done anything to help me.'

'And you betrayed her too!'

'Hello?' said John. 'I'm the big baddie, remember? Of course I did! OK. So you've foiled Phase One of my plan, the **custard hippo** bit. Big deal, guys. 'Cause now Phase Two kicks in. The real plan, which I like to call

OPERATION BOOOOM!'

'Operation Boom?' exclaimed Gemma and Arabella and Dan and Flax all together.

'No,' said John.

'OPERATION BOOOOM!

With four "o"s. Like a boom but much, much bigger!' With his horn, he levered open a small metal panel, revealing a large red button.

'Uh-oh,' said Dan. 'Something tells me this isn't going to end well.'

John thumped his pudgy hoof down on the red button. Instantly, there was a tremendous rumbling sound and the room began to shake.

Arabella looked through a tiny window and gave a gasp. 'The tower's moving!' she cried. 'This whole thing's taking off like a rocket!'

'Like a missile, actually,' said John the

unicorn, raising his voice over the roar of engines. 'I've converted this whole tower into one gigantic nuclear missile.'

'How is that even possible?' asked Flax. 'Where would you get such technology?'

John gave a chuckle. 'From Nippington Squipford, of course! It's amazing what you can pick up at a car boot sale!'

'I know I'm going to regret asking this,' said Arabella, 'but what the heck is happening? Where are we going?'

'Dandelion Grove,' said John the unicorn, pleasantly.

'Dandelion Grove?' repeated Dan. 'That sounds horrif – err – well, that sounds quite nice, actually.'

Flax shook his head. 'No, it doesn't. Dandelion Grove is a huge nuclear power station. It provides nearly ten per cent of all the country's electricity.'

Dan frowned. 'Why are we going there?'

Arabella groaned. 'We're not just going there, you hairy halfwit. We're going to crash into it! Am I right, John?'

The unicorn winked. 'Got it in one!'

'Oh,' said Dan. 'Not so nice.'

'In a mere ten minutes' time,' said John, 'this tower will crash into the Dandelion Grove nuclear power plant. The resulting explosion will release a burst of radiation so intense it will destroy every living thing within a thousand miles! Toys, however, will be unaffected! Imagine! No more people. A land ruled by toys. Paradise!'

'But you'll be blown sky high with all the rest of us when we crash,' pointed out Flax.

'Wrong, my buck-toothed friend,' sniggered

John, 'for I shall be escaping this very minute!' He pushed the window with a hoof and it swung open, letting in howling bursts of wind. 'Goodbye, you bunch of deeply stupid fools!' he yelled. He leaped out of the window and pressed a small button set into his saddle.

A parachute opened perfectly from it like a blossoming rose, and for an instant John the unicorn hung suspended outside the window.

Then a sharp gust of wind blew him back inside the control room. He bumped and skidded along the floor in a tangle of straps and lines, his long wonky horn tearing a large jagged hole in the parachute as he went.

Finally, he slid to a halt at Arabella's feet and peeped out from under torn folds of silk. 'Well,' he said quietly, 'this is awkward.'

'Can you turn this thing around?' demanded Dan. 'Land it safely?'

'It's a missile,' shrugged John. He tried desperately to free himself from the ruined parachute, grunting and wriggling, but found he was stuck fast. 'They're not really designed to land safely. They tend to be more about blowing up. Could someone please release me from this – ?'

'No chance, you conniving little pony,' interrupted Arabella.

John huffed and rested his head on the floor.

'So,' said Arabella, 'we're all stuck here on this thing until it crashes into the power plant and explodes in ten minutes?'

'Nearer eight minutes, now,' said John,

eyeing the clock, 'but otherwise, yep. That's about the size of it.'

'There must be something we can do,' said Flax, inspecting the control panel. 'Perhaps we can cut off the fuel supply somehow.'

'Don't bother,' said John. 'It's all completely hardwired and impenetrable. Not even our muscular teddy bear friend here could smash his way into the workings of this thing. That was rather a stupid suggestion, if I may say so.'

'You're an absolute ray of sunshine, you are, aren't you!' yelled Arabella. 'Here we are trying desperately to think up ways to save our lives – and the lives of everyone in the entire country – and all you do is insult us! I ought to wrap that wonky horn of yours around your neck, you numbskull nag!'

There followed a long pause, during which everyone felt thoroughly miserable.

Arabella slumped in a seat and fumed silently. She caught sight of Chloe Potty staring at her from where she and her father were tied up in the little storage room, her eyes wide and fearful. The rag doll leaped to her feet and turned to face the others. 'We need to split from this joint and then blow it up before it crashes. Flax — see if you can radio the government. Get them to send another missile to blow this one up safely in mid-air. Everyone else — search this place. Tear it apart. We need to find anything we could make a glider or parachutes out of. We haven't got long. Let's get moving. And untie Doctor Potty and Chloe! They can help!'

They dashed and jostled and hunted around the small control room, opening cupboards, lifting up panels and hatches, searching for anything that might save them.

'I've had a quick word with the army,' said Flax, cupping a paw to his radio headset. 'There's a missile on its way to us. Should take about three minutes. I know I speak for all of us here when I say:

EEEEK!'

'OK, guys and dolls,' said Arabella. 'What have we found?'

'I found a lot of canisters of helium in this cupboard,' said Dan. 'I guess they must use it to inflate kids' balloons.'

'Brilliant!' said Arabella. 'We can float to the ground on balloons!'

'Erm, the only problem is,' said Dan, 'that there aren't any balloons. Anywhere. Well, there was one left. But it was popped, so not much use.'

Arabella rolled her eyes. 'Oh, *wonderful*. Gemma, Chloe, Doctor Potty – I don't suppose you guys found any balloons, did you?'

Gemma shook her head. 'No, sorry.'

There was a long pause filled only by the sound of missile engines.

Arabella pictured the horrifying sight of the missile smashing into Dandelion Grove, popping its domed reactor building as easily as a ...

Hey, wait a minute!

'Right,' said Arabella, 'listen up, guys. I think I just had me an idea.'

CHAPTER TEN

JOSEPH MULCH GETS A BIG SURPRISE

Far above a wide expanse of fields, a pink-and-yellow tower streaked through the sky. At the very top, at the entrance to the helter-skelter slide that wound around it, stood a small, frightened rag doll.

'I'll go first,' said Arabella. 'It was my idea so I should test it.'

'I think we're beyond the testing stage,' said Dan. 'Good luck, pal.'

Arabella took a box in one hand and a canister of helium in the other. She lowered herself on to the slide and pushed.

FSshLLLOOOOOOOHHHHHH!

It was the fastest slide she had ever experienced. The freezing air rippled her hair and rattled her eyes. Around and around the slide she raced. She plunged a hand into the box, drew out a clump of sticks of bubblegum, crammed them into her mouth and chewed with all her might.

She grimaced. The taste was awful. Hair flavour? What idiot had dreamed that up?

Then she pursed her lips and blew. A bright pink bubble emerged from her mouth. Quickly, she took the bubble and carefully attached it to the nozzle of the helium canister ...

FSshLLLOOOOOOOHHHHHH!

Arabella flew off the end of the slide and into mid-air, spinning, spiralling, tumbling towards the ground at high speed ...

She pressed the release button next to the canister's nozzle.

WHHHOOOOOOSSSHHHH!

The pink bubble expanded to the size of a parachute. Instantly, Arabella sensed she was falling at a slower rate.

Soon, she was drifting gently downwards through the air like a flower petal on a summer breeze. She laughed delightedly.

There may have been no balloons in the Bubblegum Tower, but, as the Spy Toys had noticed on their climb up the tower's central staircase, there was plenty of bubblegum.

Back at the top of the helter-skelter, Dan and the others watched as Arabella descended slowly beneath them on her bubblegum balloon.

'It works!' cried Flax. 'Come on, let's all do the same. Chloe first.' He passed the young girl a stick of Neverpop Bubble Gum. 'Good luck!'

'Ha!' cried Chloe, unwrapping the gum. 'This looks like fun!' She took a canister of helium and disappeared down the slide with a cry of

'WHEEEEEEEEEEEE!'

'Erm, excuse me,' called a voice from the control room. It was John the unicorn. 'You chaps will untangle me from this parachute so I can escape, too, won't you?'

Dan rolled his eyes. 'Yeah, don't you worry, pal. We'll save a stick of gum for you. But don't even think about escaping once you land.'

One by one, they slid down the slide, inflated their pink bubbles of gum and launched themselves into the air: Doctor Potty, Gemma Snowdrop, Flax and Dan.

Finally, it was John the unicorn's turn. Left alone on the hurtling Bubblegum Tower, he wished there was something he could do to prevent it being destroyed before it hit its target. But he knew it was hopeless. Ah, well. There would be other evil plans, he promised himself. Bigger and better ones.

Maybe something involving a giant remote-controlled octopus? That might be good ...

Daydreaming, he took his stick of bubblegum and his canister of gas and stepped on to the slide. Whizzing along, he blew a nice big bubble and inflated it with the helium. But as he struggled to attach it to the canister, he accidentally popped the bubble with his horn and it collapsed around him in a soggy pink mess, pinning him to the floor of the slide.

'Gah!' he groaned. 'I hate being a unicorn.'

★ ★ ★

Drifting down gently, Arabella saw a light glow brightly in the distance. She realised it was the fiery exhaust of the army's missile thundering its way to the rescue.

Before she knew what was happening, the ground flew up to meet her with a crunching thud and she landed in the middle of a wide grassy field. Dazed, she shook her head and looked up into the sky, shielding her eyes with her hand.

Suddenly, the blazing arrow of the army missile struck the cheerful pink-and-yellow form of the Bubblegum Tower. There was a tremendous, blazing explosion that lit up the sky like a hundred suns.

★ ★ ★

At the top of a hill on the outskirts of a tiny
village called Stipple Hemlock, a tiny boy
called Joseph Mulch sat under a tree, cursing

his luck. Half an hour ago his little sister, Bethany, had fallen off a seesaw and grazed her knee. To cheer her up, he had given her his last stick of bubblegum, a stick he had been saving for weeks. He was glad Bethany had stopped crying, but he was annoyed about losing his last stick of gum. So he had come here, to the field with the hill and the tree on the edge of the farmland where he lived, which was where he usually went to sulk and ponder the unfairness of life.

He sighed – and then heard a bang.

Looking up through the branches of the tree, he saw a bright flash in the sky. And then – to his immense surprise – it began to rain sticks of bubblegum.

He was even more surprised a moment

later when a young girl floated to the ground
in front of him on a vast pink bubble.

'How – how – err – did you do that?' he stammered at her, scarcely able to believe what he was seeing.

'We were fighting an evil unicorn that wanted to wipe out the human race,' she said matter-of-factly. 'But it wasn't hard. Unicorns are such wusses.'

EPILOGUE

HAPPY ENDINGS AND ALL THAT SORT OF THING

The following Saturday, the Spy Toys once more found themselves in Auntie Roz's office. And once more, she was keeping them waiting.

Arabella suddenly stood up and announced, 'I've got better things to do than hang around here all day. I could be doing something fun like pairing my socks. Not that I own any socks. I'm strictly a tights girl. So I'd have to go shopping for some socks first and then pair them. Whaddya say, guys? Up for a little

sock shopping and then a massive pairing party?'

Before either Dan or Flax could reply – which would almost certainly have been to say something along the lines of 'Shut up, Arabella, and stop talking such total nonsense' – Auntie Roz strode briskly into the room and pressed the button that made the huge video screen slide down from the ceiling.

'Afternoon, team,' she announced (as it was the weekend, she allowed herself the luxury of this informal greeting) and consulted a diary on her smartphone. 'Why are we here today? Ah yes, debrief from the Potty mission. Happy endings and all that sort of thing. Well, no time to lose. I have an

important task for you to carry out after this.'

Arabella shook her head in disbelief. It was a nonstop life in the **DEPARTMENT OF SECRET AFFAIRS.**

'First of all,' said Auntie Roz, bringing up an image of Chloe, Doctor Potty and Gemma Snowdrop on her screen, 'a message.' She flicked a switch and the still picture became a moving image.

'Good afternoon,' said Doctor Potty, looking happier than the Spy Toys had ever seen him. 'First of all, my daughter and I wish to extend our heartiest thanks for the bravery you have shown. Don't we, Chloe?'

Chloe did not respond. She seemed to be busy playing with something that was just out of sight of the video camera filming them. Her father nudged her. 'Chloe. Thank the Spy Toys for saving the life of everyone in the country.'

Chloe sighed. 'But I'm playing!'

Arabella smirked. 'That's my girl!'

Gemma cut in. 'I think what Chloe is trying to say is thank you. Thank you so much for your extraordinary courage and quick thinking. That goes for me, too.'

'She's all right, really, that Gemma,' said Arabella. 'For some snobby doll.'

'And thank you from me,' said another voice. A blue rectangular shape wriggled into view. It was the toy that Chloe had been playing with. A rippling, writhing thing, on which was printed a picture of a tropical sunset …

'Jade the Jigsaw!' said Dan.

'I've finally found a family who want me!' said Jade.

'And she's a totally brilliant toy!' said Chloe happily. 'She doesn't mind how roughly I play with her because she can always put herself back together again!'

She pulled the jigsaw to bits, and each piece laughed wildly and sprinted off in a different direction ...

Suddenly, the video of the happy family on the screen vanished. 'That's enough of that soppy rubbish,' said Auntie Roz. 'You get the drift. Here's what happened to John the unicorn.'

A picture appeared on the screen of a greyish puddle of plastic. Protruding from it was John's long, wonky unicorn's horn, like the cone from a dropped ice cream.

'John the unicorn was mostly melted by the missile strike. He was picked up by a policebot at the scene of the wreckage. However, even as a puddle of molten plastic he still retains his devious personality, so he's been locked away in a high-security bucket at the government's secret prison for criminally insane playthings. I think that's everything, isn't it?'

'Very efficient,' said Flax. 'Now, I believe you said you had an important task for us to carry out?'

'Indeed!' beamed Auntie Roz. 'As a

thank-you for all your hard work, I have laid on a little party for you.' She pressed a button on her desk and a great quantity of party streamers and coloured balloons fell from the ceiling. Disco lights flashed and loud pop music blared.

'I know you don't actually eat and drink, but there's music and dancing and silly games to play and so forth.'

The three Spy Toys laughed in astonishment. 'Nifty!' cried Arabella. 'Very nifty!'

'You have exactly ten minutes to enjoy it,' said Auntie Roz with a smile. 'Your next mission starts directly after that. Have fun.'

Hooked on SPY TOYS?

For an exclusive sneak peek at their next daring mission, read on ...

UNDERCOVER

COMING SOON!

CHAPTER ONE

ARTHUR PARKINSON GETS A SURPRISE

The old man hurrying along the deserted street was about to have the strangest day of his life.

It was a smidgen before six o'clock on a chilly March morning. A Monday. At this hour most people are snoozing restlessly under their duvets, trying not to think about the coming week at work or school, but the old man didn't mind being up at this early hour. He was whistling a tune to himself as he walked briskly along, thinking about how lucky he was to work in a chocolate factory.

Arthur Parkinson had been caretaker at the Chimpwick's Chocolate manufacturing plant for twenty-nine years. The hours suited him, his co-workers were friendly and the factory was just a short walk from his house. He even liked that he always came home smelling of chocolate. There are worse things for a person to smell of – as his friend Haddocky Brian, who worked in the fishmongers, often complained.

This morning Arthur Parkinson was in a particularly good mood because he had a new torch. This may not sound like a big deal, but Arthur felt like a medieval knight with a brand new sword, who was just itching for a bit of stabby, dragon-slaying action to break it in. One of Arthur's main duties at the factory was fixing things – not the big, chocolate-producing machines (they were fixed automatically by robots) – but the little things: stopped taps, grumbling radiators, popped light bulbs. These were the times you needed a sturdy, reliable torch at hand, and having one always made Arthur feel he could solve any problem.

He switched the torch on and marvelled at the way its powerful whitish-yellow beam stretched far off into the morning gloom, like a long finger of light. He nodded to himself, pleased. As torches went, this was a cracker. He switched it off and stowed it securely in his coat pocket.

Above the rooftops of the town, the sky was slowly turning pink, the sun readying itself to peep over the horizon and mark the beginning of another day. Nearing the old wrought-iron factory gate, Arthur took out a weighty bunch of keys. He opened the large iron lock and pushed open the gate. As it swung open, it made the same satisfying creak it had made for the past twenty-nine years. Then Arthur stopped, frozen to the spot, his mouth slowly sagging open.

He shook his head. What he was seeing was ridiculous – or rather, what he was not seeing. *Snap out of it, Arthur,* he told himself. *Get a grip.* Heart racing, he dug in his pocket for his new torch, switched it to its brightest setting and swung the beam before him in a slow, steady arc ... But there was nothing to see. The entire Chimpwick Chocolate factory had disappeared.

HAVE YOU READ DAN, ARABELLA AND FLAX'S FIRST ADVENTURE?

Dan is a teddy bear. He's made for hugging. Aw, so cute, right? **WRONG!**

Dan's so strong he can CRUSH CARS. But what makes him a FAULTY TOY could make him the PERFECT SPY.

Together with a robot police rabbit and one seriously angry doll, Dan joins a **TOP SECRET TEAM** designed to **STOP CRIMINALS** in their tracks.

And just in time! An evil elephant hybrid is planning to kidnap the prime minister's son.

This is a job for...
SPY TOYS